Whitey, Blackie and Brownie, whom you may have met in my first book, **Three Little Horses,** became three Royal little horses. Wearing golden crowns, soft leather boots and, in cold weather, jackets and trousers, they lived in the King's Palace. "Now you are not real horses any more!" cried the other animals.

And so began the further adventures of Whitey, Blackie and Brownie, which I tell about in this book.

Piet Worm

# 3 LITTLE HORSES AT THE KING'S PALACE

by piet worm

Random House · New York

Published in New York by Random House, Inc.,

and simultaneously in Toronto, Canada, by Random House of Canada, Limited.

Library of Congress Catalog Card Number: 62-8732

Manufactured in the United States of America

To children all over
the world,
who have learned to
love
the three little horses.

Once upon a time a King, a Queen, and three little princesses lived in this Royal Palace.

And it was here that the princesses brought three dear little horses to live —Whitey, Blackie and Brownie.

A sentry on horseback stood guard in front of the Palace. When it rained, the sentry and his horse took shelter in the sentry box.

It was a dull life for the poor horse. He didn't have any fun at all.

But Whitey, Blackie and Brownie did, as you shall see!

Whitey
Blackie

For Whitey, Blackie and Brownie became Royal little horses. Like members of the Royal Family, each wore a golden crown. When they played indoors, soft leather boots were put over their hoofs. And when it was very cold, they wore jackets and trousers, like the ones Brownie has on.

Yes, the three little horses lived very well indeed. No stable for them!

The King himself had said, "We shall make an exception for these little horses. Since they are dear friends of the princesses, they shall live in the Palace."

And the Queen saw to it that special rooms were prepared for Whitey, Blackie and Brownie and that they were made as comfortable as possible. "We do want you to like it here," she told them.

How happy that made the little princesses! They asked the three little horses: "Are you happy too? Will you always stay and never leave us?"

And when the little horses, nodded, "Yes, yes," the princesses clapped their hands with joy.

All day long the little horses played in the Royal garden. Then at five o'clock a Royal servant carrying a huge clock would arrive and say, "See that? Time for your baths!"

And, lined up
in the Hall of
the Palace, were
their soft leather
boots, ready to
be put on.

Then, off came the boots again, and the three little horses were put into wooden tubs and rubbed with Royal soap and Royal sponges until they were clean from head to foot. How they enjoyed this!

After their baths, the little horses sat on small stools and, with Royal napkins tied around their necks, were served dinner by the Royal servants. The meals were always delicious, and very often there was strawberry shortcake for dessert.

They were fed from golden spoons and golden plates.

Then they were ready for bed.

They got into their pajamas and were escorted to a lovely bedroom by the little princesses.

The princesses showed the little horses the warm cozy beds that had been prepared for them, and tucked them in. Then the princesses sang this lullaby:

*Sleep, little horses, sleep,*
*Tomorrow is another day*
*Full of sunshine and happy play.*
*Sleep, little horses, sleep.*

And before the princesses had finished the song, the little horses were fast asleep.

BROWNIE
BLACKIE
WHITEY

One fine autumn day, Whitey, Blackie and Brownie were playing with the princesses in the Royal garden. Suddenly they saw a strange woman walk by, carrying a large suitcase.

"Who is she?" asked the three little horses. "Why is the servant bowing so deeply before her?"

The little princesses did not know.

But the King did. He told the Queen, "I have engaged a governess. She is to teach the little princesses reading, writing, and arithmetic."

The King greeted the governess kindly, saying: "Welcome, dear lady. We hope that the little princesses will become good students under your guidance." The princesses and Whitey, Blackie and Brownie had been peeking in through the window, but they could not hear what was being said. What did it all mean, they wondered?

Now they had to study. No more playing in the garden all day! One morning the princesses began crying.

1 + 1 =
2 + 1 =
3 + 1 =

The governess thought they were weeping because the lessons were too hard, but the little princesses said: "No, it isn't that. We miss Whitey, Blackie and Brownie."

And the little horses?

They began crying, too! "We don't see the princesses any more," they complained. "It's no fun at all playing by ourselves."

The governess saw that something had to be done. So she went to the King and told him the whole story.

And the wise King said: "Here's how to fix things. Have the little horses take lessons with the princesses!"

So Whitey, Blackie and Brownie went to school at the palace with the little princesses. Now everybody was happy! And the study hours became a pleasure because the six little friends were all learning their lessons together.

This was Whitey's first drawing. On the boat you can see the Royal Family, the three little horses, and the governess.

Don't you think Whitey did very well indeed with his first drawing? He drew the black lines first, and then put in the colors. And such lovely colors!

Yes, Whitey was a real artist.

Brownie tried to make a drawing, too. But the ink spilled all over the paper. So he thought quickly and said, "This is a night scene. It's so dark you can't see anything!"

And Blackie? Did he make a drawing? "No," he said. "I can't! I just can't draw!"

Here are some samples from Whitey's, Blackie's and Brownie's writing books. Whitey wrote:

AaBbCcDdEe

Brownie wrote:

My name is Brownie

And this is what Blackie wrote:

Blackie is my name

The governess was very pleased with her pupils. "The little horses are really wonderful!" she cried. "I never would have believed it if I hadn't seen them do it!"

And the little princesses? They did very well, too. They even wrote this long sentence:

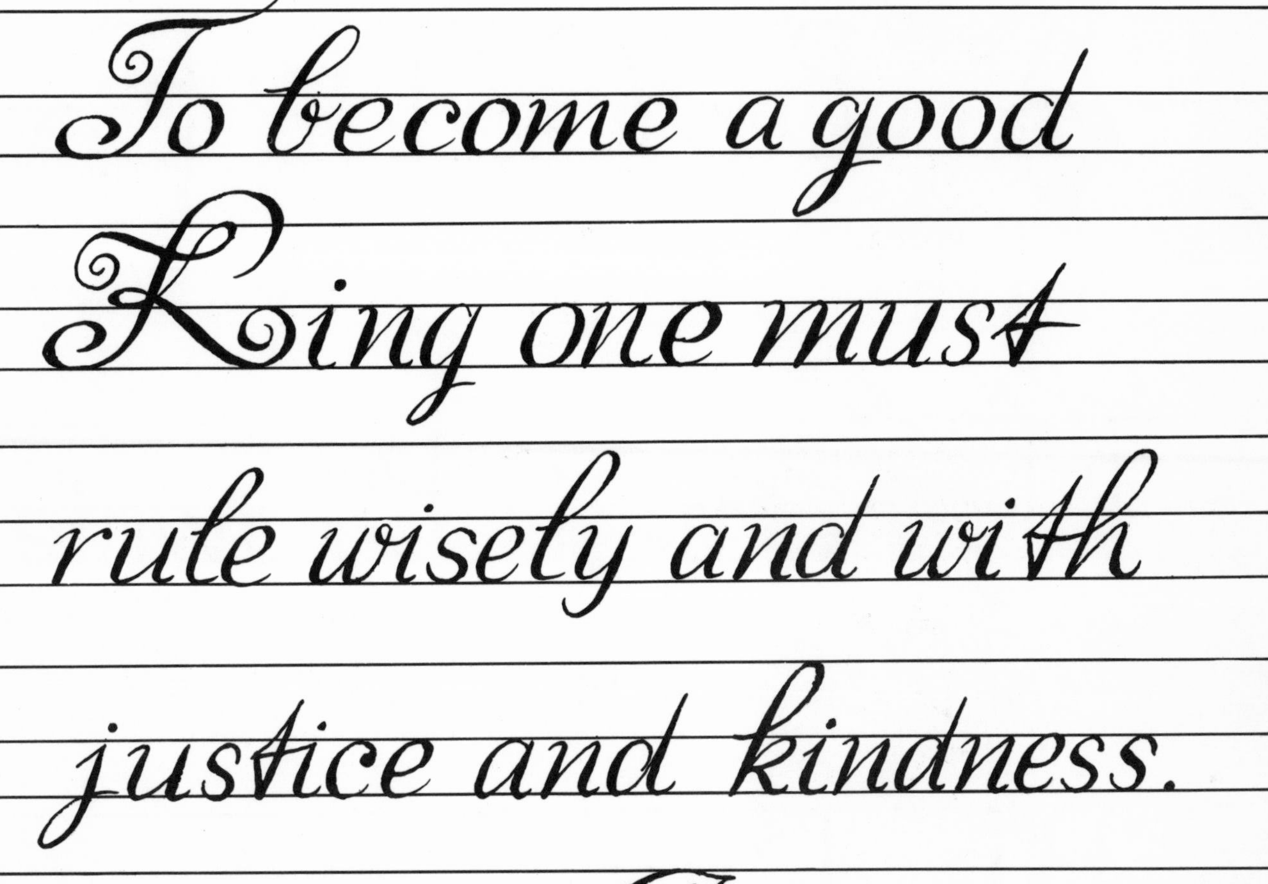

The little pupils had singing lessons, too. Their favorite song, made up by the governess, was called "Song of the Three Little Horses."

2.
We are three very peculiar Royal horses,
Sitting in class and sleeping in beds,
Wearing Royal shoes and Royal crowns
On our feet and on our heads.

LITTLE HORSES
Lyrics by the Governess.
Whitey, I'm Brownie, and Blackie is my name. We
that is our fame.
3.
We are three very charming little horses,
Who are extremely happy and oh! so gay
We sing this song like happy birds
In the sunshine in the month of May.

One fine morning Whitey,
Blackie and Brownie were
in the Palace garden.

Whitey was reading aloud from a storybook when suddenly some chickens, ducks, dogs, a cat, and a pig came by and made fun of the little horses.

"How silly you look," they said, "with crowns on your heads and dressed like that!" And then they left, still laughing.

"Do we look silly?" Whitey asked.

Brownie said, "Maybe we do."

And then they all said, "We must be real horses again! Strong horses who help people to carry heavy loads. Yes, that's what we want to be!"

That night,
Whitey, Blackie
and Brownie
opened the
window of their
bedroom and
jumped out into
the garden. They
left all their
clothes behind.
Now they looked
just like ordinary
little horses.
Their hearts were
beating fast and
there were tears
in their eyes, for
they hated to
leave the little
princesses. Yet
they had to go.

Once they were out of the garden, Whitey, Blackie and Brownie started galloping into the dark night. They had no idea where they were going. All they knew was that they had to leave the Palace. They must live like real horses again!

They wanted to go so far away that neither the King, the Queen, nor even the little princesses would find them. So they ran and ran all night long.

By the time the sun rose they were very tired.

So they dropped down onto a green meadow and soon were fast asleep.

Suddenly Whitey woke up. He had heard somebody crying. He looked around. And there, not far off, he saw . . .

. . . a fair! A real fair, with a marvelous old-fashioned merry-go-round! But why was that woman crying? And what was printed on the sign that man was putting up?

Here is what had happened:

The man and his wife, Mr. and Mrs. Lenski, who operated a merry-go-round, had lost their dear old horse, Blaze. Blaze had been the "motor" that kept the merry-go-round turning, and now that he was dead, the poor old couple had no way of earning a living.

Everybody felt sorry for the Lenskis, but nobody could think of a way to help them. The poor man and his wife were still weeping helplessly when they hung up this sign:

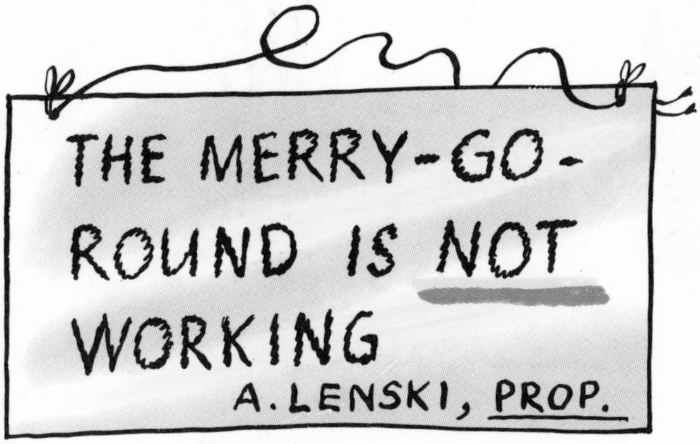

When Whitey
heard the story,
he said to Blackie and Brownie: "See here, we've got to do something to

help this poor old couple. Let's show them that we can keep their merry-go-round turning!"

Blackie was the first to do it. Mr. Lenski put the harness on him and said: "When I ring the bell, off you go! And when I shout 'Ho!' you must stop."

It was really quite simple!

While Blackie was
working, Mrs. Lenski
hugged Whitey and Brownie and gave them each a lump of sugar.

"You are so sweet," she said. "Thank you for being so helpful."

The ballet dancer praised them, too. "What darlings!" she exclaimed.

And the clown? He was so happy for Mr. and Mrs. Lenski that he played gay little tunes on his violin. His little dog, catching the spirit, began to dance, and another clown playing the saxophone came along to join in the merriment.

As for Mr. Lenski, he told the children that thanks to the three little horses, the merry-go-round was working again.

"Hurray!" the children shouted.

"It's five cents a ride," Mr. Lenski reminded them, smiling.

Everything seemed to be going well. Children were coming from all sides with money in their hands. They could not seem to wait for their turn on the old-fashioned merry-go-round.

Suddenly the little horses looked up in alarm. Then they quickly went and hid behind Mrs. Lenski. Why did they do that? And why did the ballet dancer look so upset?

There stood a gentleman-in-waiting from the Palace! The clown and Mr. Lenski were bowing to him.

"What can I do for you, sir?" Mr. Lenski asked.

And the gentleman-in-waiting said: "The Royal princesses have been heartbroken ever since their dear friends, Whitey, Blackie and Brownie, three little horses, ran away from the Palace." He told Mr. Lenski and the clown the whole story, ending with, "So, when the King heard that you were here, he said, 'When I was a little boy, a ride on the merry-go-round could always make me forget anything I was feeling unhappy about. So let's see if a lot of rides won't do the same for the little princesses.' "

Mrs. Lenski had guessed at once

that the three little horses who were working the merry-go-round were the princesses's little friends. When the gentleman-in-waiting left, promising to be back with the Royal family, she told the little horses, "Don't worry, darlings. You're safe here."

Mr. Lenski also understood the whole situation. And when Whitey, Blackie and Brownie started to explain why they had run away from the Palace, Mr. Lenski stopped them and said, "Never mind. I understand perfectly. Leave everything to me."

And without saying another word, he dragged away three wooden horses from the merry-go-round and had Whitey, Blackie and Brownie take the places of the wooden horses. Then he smiled and said, "Now stand very still, my dears!"

The Royal
Family arrived,
and Whitey,
Blackie and
Brownie stood
still while the
little princesses
climbed onto
their backs.
But who was
going to make
the merry-go-
round turn?

"Sire," Mr.
Lenski told the
King, "we'll
have to push."

So everybody
helped, including
the King and
Queen.

What fun! Suddenly one of the little princesses said, "My horse looks like Blackie!" The second one said, "Mine looks like Brownie!" and the third one said, "Mine looks like Whitey!"

Then each one cried out: "My little horse is soft and warm!"

And suddenly they knew. "They're not wooden!" they exclaimed. "They are our own dear Whitey, Blackie and Brownie!"

When the King heard this and saw how happy his little daughters were, he said: "I shall have the little horses taken back to the Palace."

At this Mr. and Mrs. Lenski became very upset, and they pleaded with the King. "Your Highnesses, the little horses are helping us to earn a living," they explained. "What would we do without them? Please let them stay with us!"

When the King and Queen understood how badly the poor old couple needed the three little horses, they graciously consented to let them keep them.

The little princesses agreed that it was the right thing to do. "We must all help one another," they said.

And they had something to look forward to, for Whitey, Blackie and Brownie promised to come to the Palace every year on the little princesses' birthday.

So the Royal family went back to the Palace, and the three little horses continued working the merry-go-round. They enjoyed doing it and stayed with Mr. and Mrs. Lenski for a long time, going from village to village and making all the children in the kingdom very happy.